THE PUPPY PLACE

PUGSLEY

ELLEN MILES

A
LITTLE APPLE
PAPERBACK

SCHOLASTIC INC.

New York   Toronto   London   Auckland   Sydney
Mexico City   New Delhi   Hong Kong   Buenos Aires

For Eileen (With thanks for the inspiration),

and Ava Rose.

ISBN-13: 978-0-545-03455-5
ISBN-10: 0-545-03455-8

Cover art by Tim O'Brien
Designed by Steve Scott

12 11 10   10 11 12/0

Printed in the U.S.A.

First printing, September 2007

CHAPTER ONE

Dogs.

Dogs.

Dogs.

Everywhere Lizzie Peterson looked, she saw dogs. Huge dogs and tiny dogs, curly-haired dogs and long-eared dogs, and dogs with big, fluffy tails. There were dogs that barked and dogs that whined and dogs that ran across the floor with their toenails clicking and their mouths wide open in huge doggy smiles.

Lizzie was in heaven. She didn't know which dog to hug first, which one to pat, which one to tell, "Good dog!" So she tried to do it all. She leaned over to hug a big, gentle shepherd mix, held out a hand to pat the pushy nose of a white-and-brown terrier, and said, "Happy Birthday, Max!" to the goofy black Lab who had brought over a stuffed clown to show her. It was Max's birthday (he was turning two), and Lizzie had been helping to set up a doggy birthday party for him.

"You sure do love dogs," said the woman standing next to Lizzie.

"I sure do," Lizzie said, reaching out to pat another dog who had run over to visit.

Lizzie smiled up at her aunt Amanda, the owner of Bowser's Backyard. Aunt Amanda was tall and thin with long, curly red hair. She didn't look much at all like Lizzie's dad, even though she was his little sister. Aunt Amanda and her husband, Uncle James, had lived in California for the last ten years, so Lizzie had hardly ever met them, except at one family reunion.

Of course, Lizzie had heard lots of stories about "dog-crazy Amanda," but she'd never had a chance to get to know her aunt. That is, not until Aunt Amanda and Uncle James had moved to Littleton.

Aunt Amanda had just opened her dream business: a doggy day care. And it wasn't far from Lizzie's house!

"And dogs love *you*, too," her aunt added now. "I can see that. You really have a way with animals."

Lizzie felt like she might burst with happiness. Coming from Aunt Amanda, that meant a lot.

Lizzie had been stopping by Bowser's Backyard at least once a week since it had opened. It was the first doggy day care business in Littleton. At first, Lizzie wasn't even sure what doggy day care *was*.

Aunt Amanda had explained that it was a place where people could bring their dogs for the day. The dogs could play safely there all day and get to know other dogs. Then their owners didn't have to leave them home alone while they (the people, that is!) went to work. With the help of her staff, Amanda cared for up to thirty dogs a day — including her own dogs.

She and Uncle James had two adorable pugs named Lionel and Jack, plus a sweet old golden retriever named Bowser. Lizzie had never known a pug before, but as soon as she met Lionel and Jack she understood why Aunt Amanda was "pug crazy," as she called it. The two pugs were like little brown bundles of energy, with flat wrinkly faces and curly corkscrew tails. And they were cuddly, too. They were the funniest, cutest dogs Lizzie had ever met.

Lizzie liked to talk about dogs — any kind of dogs, not just pugs — with Aunt Amanda. Of course, her aunt already knew all about how Lizzie and her family took care of puppies that needed homes. They kept them only until they found the perfect forever home for each one. The Petersons loved being a foster family.

Lizzie also told Aunt Amanda about how she volunteered once a week at Caring Paws, the animal shelter. One day, Lizzie worked up the courage to ask Aunt Amanda for a job. "I have lots of experience," she'd said. "I know a lot about dogs, but there's a lot more I want to learn." Lizzie knew she was too young for a real job, but even a fourth grader like her could be a lot of help when it came to taking care of thirty dogs! "I'll do anything!" she had said. "You don't even have to pay me. I just want to be here."

"And I love having you here," Aunt Amanda had said. "You're a big help. How about this? We'll start with one afternoon a week. Once we see how things work out, maybe you can come more often."

And now, on Lizzie's very first day, Aunt Amanda was smiling at Lizzie and telling her what a good job she was already doing. "I can see you'll be a good helper, Lizzie. I may even need you to come up to Camp Bowser with me one weekend, if we have a lot of campers."

Camp Bowser! Lizzie couldn't believe her ears. Ever since she had first heard about Camp Bowser, Lizzie had wanted to go there. What could be more fun than a sleepaway camp for dogs? When Aunt Amanda and Uncle James had moved from California, they'd also bought a cabin in the country. Every weekend they took five or six dogs along when they went up to their country place. The dogs could run around in a big fenced area, swim in the brook, or even do arts and crafts, just like kids at a regular camp.

Going to Camp Bowser would be — well, it would be the best thing that ever happened to Lizzie!

Well, maybe the best thing next to getting Buddy. Lizzie smiled as she thought of the little brown puppy that had come to live with her family. The Petersons had fostered lots of puppies, and Lizzie and her brothers, Charles and the Bean (whose real name was Adam), had wanted to keep every single one. But Mom and Dad said that the Petersons weren't ready for a full-time dog. The Bean was just a toddler, and he needed lots of attention. Plus, Mom was more of a cat person.

Then Buddy came along. The Petersons were caring for four dogs at that time. Lizzie had met a mother dog named Skipper plus her three puppies, Cinnamon, Cocoa, and Buddy, at the shelter. Cinnamon and Cocoa, the girl puppies, were very cute, and Lizzie was thrilled when they found forever homes.

But it was different with Buddy. Buddy was special. He was a small puppy, the runt of his litter. He needed lots of love and attention. Everyone fell in love with Buddy: Lizzie, Charles, the Bean, Dad, and even — especially! — Mom. And when the time came to find Buddy a forever home, the Petersons all agreed that he would stay right there with them. Now Buddy was a part of the family.

Buddy had gotten a little bigger, but he was still the cutest, sweetest pup Lizzie had ever met. She loved his soft puppy fur and his silky ears, and she loved to kiss the little white heart-shaped marking on his chest. Lizzie loved to take Buddy for walks and to teach him new tricks — his latest was "roll over" — and she loved just lying with him on the couch, patting him while she read a favorite book. Lizzie loved *everything* about Buddy.

But could Lizzie say good-bye to Buddy for a weekend, while she went to Camp Bowser with Aunt Amanda and Uncle James? Well, as long as she knew he would be there waiting for her when she got back, yes, she could.

"Wow," she said now to Aunt Amanda. "I would *love* to come to Camp Bowser."

"Well, we'll see," her aunt said. "Right now, we have some doggy guests arriving for our party. Want to help me get them settled?"

Lizzie got to her feet and dusted off her hands. "Absolutely," she said.

Just then, the door to the play area opened. "Amanda, they're here!" called Josie, one of the other helpers.

Four dogs came through the door, into the

indoor play area where Lizzie and her aunt were waiting. A golden retriever that looked just like Bowser walked in slowly, sniffing the air. A black-and-tan mutt ambled along behind her, shaking his long droopy ears. A cocoa-brown poodle tip-toed along elegantly, looking this way and that. And then, *zoom*! Lizzie laughed as she watched a little brown-and-black dog blast by the others and scamper around the play area, zipping from the jungle gym to the slide to the seesaw and back around. It was a pug! He snuffled and snorted and wagged his curly tail. He made three circles before he even paused to sniff Lizzie's out-stretched hand.

"Awww!" she said, bending to pat the dog's velvety black ears. He was just a puppy, really. His tan body shivered with joy as he licked her fingers. "Who's this?" she asked Aunt Amanda.

Aunt Amanda rolled her eyes and shook her head — but she was smiling. "This," she said, "is Pugsley. Otherwise known as Mr. Pest."

CHAPTER TWO

"Pugsley!" Lizzie laughed out loud. "What a great name. And he's such a cutie!" Lizzie could not get over how soft Pugsley's ears were. She loved the sweet expression on his wrinkled face.

Aunt Amanda rolled her eyes. "Sure, he's cute," she said. "You know I'm pug crazy. But my Jack and Lionel are well-trained little gentlemen. Pugsley is . . ." Aunt Amanda paused. "Well, there's a reason his nickname is Mr. Pest. Pugsley is a handful; let's just leave it at that."

"But Pugsley is only a puppy, right?" Lizzie asked. She was still petting his ears, but Pugsley was watching Josie put a party hat that said BIRTHDAY BOY on Max's head. The pug's strong little body started to quiver with excitement.

I like that hat. I want *that hat. I'm going to* get *that hat. Just wait until I get a chance. Watch me! Watch me! Watch me!*

Aunt Amanda nodded. "He's only about six months old," she said. "And his owners love him. But they haven't done much in the way of training, and it shows. He's house-trained, but that's about it. And he's always misbehaving. The best thing to do is just ignore him when he's acting out. He's — "

Just then, Pugsley ducked away from Lizzie's hand and took off like a little brown rocket, making a beeline for Max. He barely slowed down as he approached the bigger dog, leaped up to grab the birthday hat in his teeth, and kept moving, barreling along toward the door.

"Pugsley!" Amanda yelled. "Bring that back, you little — "

Josie ran to the door to make sure it was shut. "He can't get out," she called.

"Don't count on that," Amanda said. She turned to Lizzie. "Mr. Pest has escaped four times since he started coming here. You really have to keep an eye on him."

"What about 'three strikes and you're out'?" Lizzie asked. She knew that Aunt Amanda had a strict policy about bad behavior. Just like in baseball, every dog was allowed three strikes: three chances to mess up. But if a dog got more than three strikes by being mean to another dog or to a person, by running away or stealing from other dogs, or breaking any of Aunt Amanda's other rules, that dog would not be allowed anymore at Bowser's.

Aunt Amanda blushed. "Well," she admitted, "I guess I have a soft spot for pugs. And there's something about that Pugsley. He's a rascal, but he's so cute. I keep giving him extra chances."

At the moment, Lizzie could see that Pugsley had dashed into the nap room, which was full of cozy corners for sleepy dogs. There were bunk beds and soft round doggy beds, and three old couches with fleecy bedspreads on them. Some of the older dogs liked to spend most of their time in the nap room, snoozing the day away while the other dogs played and ran around.

The nap room was a quiet, calm place. Until Pugsley blasted in, that is. He bounced from bed to bed, waking up every sleeping dog with his sharp little barks. He jumped right onto the nose of Hoss, the Great Dane, who liked to spend his days napping on the couch.

Wake up! Wake up! Let's go have some fun! Look at this hat I found!

"It's like he's telling them it's time for the party!" Lizzie said, giggling as she watched. Hoss did not seem to think it was quite so funny.

Aunt Amanda was trying to hide a smile. "Well, I guess he's right!" she said. "It's definitely party time. Let's get everyone outside for games and cake." She caught Pugsley and pulled Max's birth-day hat out of his mouth. Lizzie noticed that her aunt also snuck in a little kiss on Pugsley's nose.

Lizzie helped round up the dogs and move them toward the back door, which opened into a fenced-in play area. It wasn't easy to get all the dogs to go to one place. Some dogs were eager to be outside and ran out with happy barks and wagging tails. But other dogs seemed confused about where to go, or just wanted to stay inside. Hoss, the Great Dane, kept circling back to the nap room.

Aunt Amanda laughed. "It's like herding cats," she said, shaking her head.

Lizzie wasn't sure what that meant — until she tried to imagine dealing with a bunch of yowling, stubborn, minds-of-their-own kitties. Dogs were bad enough! How would you *ever* get cats to do what you wanted? She laughed, too. "I'll get Hoss," she said. "It sounds like the party is starting with or without us!"

From outside came the sound of balloons popping and dogs yipping and howling. When Lizzie finally dragged Hoss out the door, she saw what was going on. Pugsley, the adorable little brat, was stealing balloons as fast as Josie could blow them up. Then he was bumping them away, using his head like a soccer player heading the ball — except that most soccer players don't follow up by belly-flopping on top of the ball until it bursts.

Every time a balloon popped, Max the birthday boy would squirm farther under the cake table, knocking his bright blue BIRTHDAY BOY hat until it was sticking straight out sideways. Which looked very silly. Which made Josie and Amanda and Lizzie crack up. Which made Pugsley so happy and excited that he would steal another balloon and repeat the whole routine.

Wheee! What fun! Come on, everybody! What are you waiting for? This is the best game ever!

"Oh, dear," Amanda said, still giggling. "I don't want to laugh, but I can't help myself. Lizzie, can you pick up those broken balloons? We have to be very careful to make sure nobody thinks they're today's special snack."

Amanda cooked something special every single day for the dogs at the Backyard. Sometimes she roasted a turkey or baked liver brownies. Lizzie knew that regular brownies could be bad for dogs, since chocolate can make dogs sick. But liver brownies were okay, and, although Lizzie couldn't imagine eating one herself, the dogs *loved* them. They also loved Amanda, and, for the most part, they listened to her and obeyed her.

All but Pugsley. Over the next three weeks, Lizzie got to know Pugsley very well. She could not believe how much trouble that little dog could get into. Lizzie worked at Bowser's Backyard every Wednesday, and Pugsley was on his worst behavior every time she saw him. He was always cute, always funny, always very entertaining — but also always very, very naughty.

One Friday afternoon, Lizzie had stopped by Bowser's Backyard to see if she could help out. That's how she happened to be cleaning up a doggy mess just outside Aunt Amanda's office when one of Pugsley's owners, a man named Ken, came to drop him off.

"You know," Lizzie heard Amanda say to Ken, "I really can't keep stretching the rules for Pugsley. If he doesn't improve his behavior soon —"

Ken interrupted her. "I know, I know," he said. "You've been so patient. But if you haven't been able to get him on the right track, I don't know who can. He's such a handful, and we just don't know what to do anymore." He was quiet for a moment. Then he let out a big sigh. "In fact," he said, "this will be the last day you have to stretch the rules. We've decided to give Pugsley up, and we're taking him to the animal shelter tomorrow."

CHAPTER THREE

"No!" Lizzie cried. Then she covered her mouth. After all, she was eavesdropping. It wasn't right to listen to other people's conversations. Her parents had taught her that. But it wasn't as if she had been listening on purpose! Still, it was probably better to keep her mouth shut. Nobody had asked her opinion.

Luckily, Ken did not seem to hear her. He left a few minutes later, after kissing Pugsley good-bye. Pugsley stood very still for once, watching his owner walk away. Lizzie could hardly bear the sad look in the pug's big brown eyes. She scooped him up and gave him a big kiss. Then she put him down. "Go play, sweetie," she said. "Don't worry. We love you."

Aunt Amanda came out of her office and saw how upset Lizzie looked. "I guess you heard that," she said.

Lizzie stared down at her shoes and nodded. "Sorry. I didn't mean to eavesdrop."

"That's okay." Aunt Amanda sighed. "But I can tell you feel the same way about Pugsley that I do. He may be a pest, but he's a sweetie, too. I don't want him to have to go to the shelter."

Lizzie shook her head. "Me, neither. I mean, I volunteer there, and it's a great place. Ms. Dobbins loves dogs as much as you do. But there are a *lot* of dogs at Caring Paws, and not enough staff to give them the attention they deserve."

"I know," said Aunt Amanda. "Plus, at least the dogs that stay with us during the day get to go home at night to comfy beds and loving owners. The dogs at the shelter sleep alone, in their kennels. That makes me sad."

Lizzie saw Aunt Amanda's eyes filling with tears and knew that she was picturing the lonely dogs at the shelter. She felt her own eyes fill up. Lizzie could remember so many times when she had left the shelter at the end of the day feeling so, so sorry for all the dogs she could not take home with her.

But then Aunt Amanda shook her head. "Still, I just can't let Pugsley drive all the other dogs crazy. Did you see him stealing everybody's toys last time you were here? He kept stashing them over behind the slide. There must have been ten toys over there by the end of the day!"

Lizzie nodded. "I saw," she said. She had also seen Max and another dog, Ruby, sniffing all over, looking for their toys. Mr. Pest was a trouble-maker, no doubt about it.

But still.

Pugsley was just a puppy. And he didn't know any better because nobody had ever taught him the *right* way to behave. Maybe she, Lizzie, could help Pugsley become a dog that somebody would be happy to own. "What if I tried to train him a little bit, during the days when I'm here?" she asked Aunt Amanda.

Aunt Amanda shook her head. "I think Ken is serious about giving him up," she said. "Pugsley won't be coming here anymore." She put her hand on Lizzie's shoulder. "I know you care," she said. "So do I. But there's really nothing we can do. Let's go see what everybody's up to. I think it's time for some outdoor play."

Lizzie tried to smile. She loved taking the dogs outside to the fenced play yard out in back. "Can Pugsley come?" she asked.

"Of course!" Aunt Amanda smiled back. "What fun would it be without Mr. Pest?" Then her smile faded.

Lizzie knew what Aunt Amanda was thinking. And she agreed. Bowser's Backyard just would not be the same without Pugsley around. Yes, it would be calmer. But it would not be as much fun. Aunt Amanda was right.

"She's right, isn't she, Mr. Pest?" Lizzie said,

when she found the pug in the nap room. He was quiet for once, curled up with Hoss on the bottom bunk. They looked so cute together! Lizzie sat down for a moment to pat the tiny pug and the gigantic Great Dane. They made such a funny pair!

Aunt Amanda had told Lizzie that when she first opened Bowser's Backyard she thought it would be a good idea to separate the big dogs from the little ones. But the dogs wanted to be together! They whined at the gates that kept them apart until Aunt Amanda gave up and let them all mingle. From then on, big dogs and little dogs wrestled, played, and napped together without any problems at all.

Now, when Lizzie started petting Pugsley, he jumped up and started sneezing. Lizzie laughed. Between Aunt Amanda's two pugs and this pup, she was getting used to typical pug behavior. They were such cuddle-bugs, all of them! They just loved to be hugged and petted. And pugs were always snuffling, snorting, and sneezing. "Anything with an S!" as Aunt Amanda said. Their funny flat faces were always in motion, and their big bulgy eyes didn't miss a thing.

"Ahh! Pugsley! Cut it out!" Now the pup had climbed up onto Lizzie's lap and was licking her face all over, snuffling softly as his curly tail wagged and wagged.

She likes it! She likes it! I can tell. She thinks I'm the funniest. Because I am! I'm the funniest! I'm the funniest dog ever! Watch this! I'll lick her some more and make her laugh even louder.

Lizzie was laughing so hard, she could hardly catch her breath. She gathered the pup in her arms. "Come on, you! It's time to go outside. You, too, Hoss!" She gave the big Great Dane a nudge. Groaning a little, he got to his feet, stretched, and stepped slowly down off the bed.

Outside, Lizzie put Pugsley down and watched

with a smile as he tore around the playground. He dashed and darted in and out among the other dogs, yipping at this one and jumping on that one and nipping at another one's chin — until the whole pack was milling around excitedly.

Yeah, that's it! Let's have some fun! Watch how it's done. First you run here, then you run there! Then you grab a toy and shake it! Then you pounce on a friend! Watch! See? Then you run here again, and there again, and grab a toy again and pounce again! Wheee!

Lizzie shook her head as she watched. Pugsley sure did know how to have a good time — and he wanted everybody else to enjoy themselves, too. He might be a handful, but he was a happy handful. Suddenly, Lizzie knew she could not say good-bye to the silly little pup.

"Aunt Amanda," Lizzie said as they stood watching the dogs play. "What if — what if my family fostered Pugsley? Would you let him keep coming to Bowser's Backyard?"

Aunt Amanda turned to stare at Lizzie. "You would take him?"

Lizzie nodded. "Just temporarily, of course. You know Dad would say yes. I'll just have to talk Mom into it," she said. "I think Pugsley would be a lot happier with us than he would be at the shelter. We can help train him and find him a good forever home."

Aunt Amanda crossed her arms. "Wow," she said. "Well, what can I say? If you're willing to take on Mr. Pest, how can I say no to him coming here whenever you're working? And — maybe, if everything works out, he could even come to Camp Bowser with us."

"Deal," said Lizzie, sticking out her hand.

"Deal," said Aunt Amanda.

They shook on it.

"Now," Lizzie said, "all I have to do is convince Mom."

CHAPTER FOUR

"You're talking about Pugsley, right?" Mom sounded amazed. "Otherwise known as Mr. Pest? The dog you said causes all sorts of trouble? The nutty little pug puppy you've been telling us about? Do you think I'm *crazy*? Or are *you* crazy?"

"Well . . ." Lizzie was sitting in Aunt Amanda's office, where she'd gone to call Mom. She could see out the big window into the indoor play area. All the dogs were inside now, and Aunt Amanda was trying to calm them down. Their owners would be coming soon to pick them up, and nobody liked driving home with a hyped-up hound.

Pugsley wasn't helping matters. He was still zooming around, trying to get everyone to play. Josie was trying to catch him, but somehow he kept squirting out of her grip. Lizzie couldn't help giggling a little as she watched.

"Well, what?" her mother asked over the phone. "And what's so funny?"

"Actually," Lizzie confessed, "it's Pugsley. I'm watching him right now. You're right, he does cause a little trouble sometimes. But he is so, so cute. You'll fall in love with him just like I have, I promise."

"Love is not the issue," her mom said sternly. "I happen to like our house, and I don't want it destroyed."

"Pugsley isn't destructive," Lizzie said. At least, she didn't *think* he was. She had never seen him pull all the stuffing out of a toy the way Max was always doing, or scratch at the door the way Fiona the poodle did. "He just likes to play, that's all. He'll be great company for Buddy. And the Bean will love him."

"I just wish we had time to talk this over as a family," Mom said. She sighed. "But I understand.

If we don't take him today, he's going to the shelter tomorrow, right?"

"That's right." Lizzie crossed her fingers and held her breath.

"And his owners have agreed to let us foster him?"

Aunt Amanda had already called Ken for permission. He was very happy to hear that Pugsley might be going to a foster family. "Yup."

Mom sighed again. "Okay. I'm willing to give Pugsley a chance. But you'll have to promise to —"

But Lizzie had jumped up from her seat and was dancing around the office, grinning. She wasn't even listening anymore. She could guess exactly what Mom was saying about taking responsibility and all that. Of *course* Lizzie would take responsibility. Hadn't she and Charles been very responsible with all the other puppies they had fostered?

"Sure, Mom, sure," she said, when she'd danced herself back over to the phone. "So, Aunt Amanda will drop me and Pugsley off in an hour or so. I can't wait for you to meet him!" She hung up before her mom could say another word.

Pugsley was not exactly on his best behavior during the ride home. Aunt Amanda had put him in the way-back of the "Bowser Mobile," the special van she used for picking up and dropping off dogs. The van was big and red and its license plate read POOCHES. Inside there were cages for eight dogs — or more, if some were small.

Right now, Aunt Amanda's pugs, Lionel and Jack, were sharing one of the cages, while her golden retriever, Bowser, took up another. Fiona the poodle was in a third; she was going to Camp Bowser for the weekend. Lizzie was jealous. She wished *she* were going to Camp Bowser. But maybe she and Pugsley would be going sometime very, very soon.

Pugsley had a cage all to himself. Lizzie would have thought he would be ready for a nap by then — after all, he'd had a long afternoon of running and playing! But no. Mr. Pest still wanted to play. He bounced from side to side in his cage, barking constantly and poking his paw into the other dogs' cages. Lizzie and Amanda did their best to ignore him, hoping his rowdy behavior would stop.

At a stoplight, Aunt Amanda looked over at Lizzie and raised her eyebrows. "Sure you're up for this?"

Lizzie could barely hear her over Pugsley's barking. She just nodded. *She* was. She just wasn't sure about the rest of her family.

She shouldn't have worried about Charles and Dad and the Bean. *They* loved Pugsley the minute they saw him. When Aunt Amanda opened the back door of the van and unlatched his cage, Pugsley poked his little wrinkled face out and sneezed. Then, as soon as Aunt Amanda put him down on the ground, he ran right over to Charles and Dad, who were standing in the front yard, and put his paws up on Charles's knees.

"Pugsley!" said Amanda. "No jumping!"

But Charles was laughing. "Ha! Nice to meet you!" he said. He knelt down and Pugsley started licking his face all over while Charles just laughed and laughed.

Dad cracked up, too. He sat down next to Charles and let Pugsley lick his face. "Well, you sure are a cutie," Dad said. "And I've heard such terrible things about you. They can't possibly be true!" Pugsley wriggled his whole body and kept licking. Dad laughed some more.

The Bean came toddling over. "Uppy!" he said, holding out a hand. He laughed his funny googly laugh. Dogs seemed to love the Bean. Maybe that was because the Bean liked to pretend he *was* a dog. He often took naps on a dog bed, and lately his favorite toy was one of Buddy's hand-me-downs, a purple starfish that squeaked.

"Hold on," Lizzie told the Bean. "Let's make sure the 'uppy' is ready to meet you." She knew it was always a good idea to take things slowly when it came to toddlers and dogs. But before she could do anything the Bean was already getting his face licked. He laughed even louder.

"Well, it looks like they'll get along," said Mom, who had come outside. She was holding Buddy on a leash.

When Pugsley saw Buddy, he wriggled out of Charles's arms and went flying over to say hello to the little brown puppy.

Hi! Hi! Hi! I like you! Do you like me? Let's play!

Buddy looked surprised for a moment. But then he started tugging on the leash as if he wanted to run around with Pugsley.

"Let's take them out in back and let them run around in the yard," Lizzie suggested.

"Sounds like a good idea," said Aunt Amanda, who was still standing near the van, watching the whole scene.

"Can you stay for dinner?" Dad asked.

32

"No, we're heading to the country," Aunt Amanda said. "I should be on my way. Anyway, it looks as if Pugsley is off to a very good start in his new home."

"New *temporary* home," Mom corrected her. But she was smiling as she looked down at Pugsley.

Lizzie felt sure that everything would work out just fine.

CHAPTER FIVE

"Is it Wednesday yet?" Mom pushed the hair off her forehead and let out an exasperated sigh.

Charles gave her a strange look. "Mom! That's silly. It's only Saturday night!"

"She knows," Lizzie told her brother. She looked from her mom to Pugsley, who was chasing his tail in the middle of the kitchen floor. Since Friday, when Pugsley had come to stay, it did seem as if a *lot* more than twenty-four hours had passed. And next Wednesday, the day when Pugsley would be allowed to spend some time at Bowser's Backyard, did seem very, very far off. Lizzie could tell her mom was already eager for a break from all-Pugsley-all-the-time.

To be honest, so was Lizzie.

Pugsley had more than lived up to his nickname. What a pest! He was constantly getting into trouble, stirring up trouble, looking for trouble, or making trouble. Well, maybe he had slept for a few hours here and there. Usually on the couch, which was the one place Mom had said she really did *not* want him to sleep.

And of course, before he could curl up for a nap on the couch, Pugsley had to throw each and every one of the couch pillows to the floor, then pounce on each one in turn, *grrr*-ing and snarling, to teach them a lesson. What was the lesson? Nobody knew. Nobody but Pugsley.

Pugsley had kept Lizzie on the run all day. If she wasn't petting him or playing with him, he would run off and get into all sorts of mischief. Whenever she took her eyes off him for even one minute, he would do something bad. Like on Friday night. Only a couple of hours after Pugsley had arrived, Lizzie was on the phone telling her friend Maria all about Mr. Pest. "Hold on," Lizzie had said suddenly, looking around, "where *is* he, anyway?"

Lizzie ran through the downstairs rooms. As she rounded the staircase, she heard snorty growling noises coming from above. She dashed up the stairs. "Pugsley!" she said. "Oh, no!"

Lizzie found Mr. Pest standing in Charles's room, looking up at her with innocent eyes.

What? Did I do something wrong?

The little dog was surrounded by a sea of wrinkled clothes that he had pulled from the neat stack of clean laundry Dad had left on Charles's bed. A pair of underpants drooped from his jaw.

Lizzie folded her arms.

Pugsley wagged his tail and opened his mouth, and the underwear fell on top of the pile.

"Argh!" Lizzie said, remembering what Aunt Amanda said about ignoring bad behavior. It was too late to punish Pugsley now, anyway. The deed was done.

By the time Lizzie had finished picking up the laundry and sorting it into two piles — "still mostly clean" and "needs another washing" — Pugsley had slipped off again.

Lizzie caught Pugsley as he dashed out of the bathroom, holding the end of a long, long, *long* ribbon of toilet paper. "You!" Lizzie cried. "You are in big trouble, Mr. — "

Watch this! Watch this! Did you ever see any-thing so funny? Look at the way it just keeps coming and coming and coming. . . .

Pugsley gave her that big-eyed innocent look again.

Then he took off down the stairs, trailing the toilet paper all the way into the living room before the roll rattled itself empty. While Lizzie wadded up the paper, Pugsley entertained himself by dashing in huge circles through the downstairs rooms. He did three laps, then he reversed direction and did three more laps the other way.

"Lizzie!" Mom yelled from the den, where she was trying to pay some bills.

"I know, Mom!" Lizzie called back. Her voice was muffled by the giant tangle of toilet paper in her arms. "I'll grab him in a sec!"

And that was just Friday night.

On Saturday, Pugsley ate some of Mom's expensive lemon-scented soap and then burped lemon-scented bubbles all day long.

On Sunday, he tore the stuffing out of every single one of Buddy's toys.

On Monday, he ate the mail before Mom or Dad could read it.

And on Tuesday, Mr. Pest jumped right *splash* into the tub while Lizzie was helping Mom give the Bean his bath.

What a naughty puppy!

The only time he was good was when Lizzie was giving him her full attention, like when she held him and petted him by the fireplace. At times like that, Pugsley was relaxed and happy and quiet.

When Wednesday finally really did arrive and she and Pugsley were at Bowser's Backyard, Lizzie listed Pugsley's crimes for Aunt Amanda.

"Oh, dear," said Aunt Amanda. "I bet your mother isn't very happy about that." She shook her head.

Lizzie thought she saw a tiny smile on her aunt's lips. "It's not funny!" she said, even though she knew that some of the things Pugsley had done were pretty hilarious. "If he keeps acting this way, Mom won't let him stay with us. And we'll never find him a forever home. Mom had a friend at work who thought she might like a pug, but when she came over to meet Pugsley, he jumped up and licked her all over. Then he ate the handles off her purse while she and Mom were having coffee. She left in a big hurry. Mom was *not* happy."

Aunt Amanda's smile disappeared. "You're right," she said. "It's serious. Pugsley has *got* to learn to behave."

Lizzie felt a knot forming in the middle of her stomach. "What about Camp Bowser?" she asked in a tiny voice. She already knew the answer.

Aunt Amanda shook her head. "Well," she said, "I was hoping for your help this weekend, since I have six dogs coming up. But Mr. Pest is not invited. I can't deal with a handful like him on top of everything else."

Lizzie's heart sank. She didn't even have to ask. She already knew the answer. She wasn't invited, either. If Pugsley had to stay home, so did she. Even if it meant missing out on going to Camp Bowser, something Lizzie was dying to do. After all, she had promised to be responsible for the little pug puppy.

CHAPTER SIX

Lizzie's friend Maria came over after school on Thursday. During the walk home, Lizzie gave Maria the Pugsley update. "This morning when I went to put on my sneakers, I couldn't find them. I had to look all over the house," she said. "Finally I found the right one in the laundry room, wedged under the dryer. The left one was in the Bean's room, under a pile of toys. And both of them were pretty chewed up." She held up one foot for Maria to see and waggled her big toe through a hole in her sneaker. "I know it wasn't Buddy who did it. He got over his chewing phase a long time ago."

Maria groaned. "Mr. Pest. That nickname is perfect for him. I never heard of such a naughty puppy."

"What am I going to do?" Lizzie asked. "No way is Mom going to let him stay much longer if he doesn't quit being so bad." Lizzie had stayed up late the night before, paging through all her puppy and dog training books. She couldn't find a single idea about how to deal with Pugsley. Most of the books said the same thing Amanda did: "Ignore bad behavior." That did not seem to work with Mr. Pest.

"I don't have a clue," Maria said. "Simba was already pretty well-trained when we got him."

Simba, a big yellow Labrador retriever, was Maria's mother's guide dog. Maria's mom was blind, but having Simba to help meant she could go just about anywhere and do just about anything that anybody else could do.

When Simba was a tiny puppy he had lived with a family who helped him grow up and learn basic manners. Then he went to guide dog school to learn how to cross busy roads, move through a crowd, and — most important — lie very quietly and patiently when he wasn't needed. Simba had come to live with the Santiagos when he was about two years old, and by then he was a very, very good dog.

"I can tell you one thing," Lizzie said. "Pugsley will probably *never* be as well-behaved as Simba." They were walking up the porch stairs at Lizzie's house, and Lizzie could already hear Pugsley inside, barking his head off.

Buddy never barked when Lizzie came home from school. He knew her footsteps and he would be waiting at the door. His tail would be wagging and he would have a silly doggy smile on his face. Lizzie had to admit that sometimes — usually, in fact — Buddy would jump up on her because he was so eager to say hello. But still, he would not be barking.

"Argh!" Lizzie said, rolling her eyes at her friend. "Mr. Pest is driving me crazy!"

The front door opened before Lizzie's hand even reached the knob. "This dog is driving me crazy!"

said her mother. She stood there holding Pugsley out at arm's length. He was wearing his little red collar, and a matching red leash dangled from it. "Take him away for a few hours. Please! I need a break."

Lizzie scooped Pugsley into her arms and nuzzled the top of his head. He snorted. Then he sneezed. And he licked her chin. At least he wasn't barking anymore. Lizzie knew better than to argue with her mother. After all, she was the one who had begged to foster Pugsley. "We'll go down to the park for a little while," she said. "Should we take Buddy along?"

"To tell you the truth," Mom said, "I think Buddy could use a Pugsley break, too." She handed Maria some granola bars and a bottle of juice. "Here's your after-school snack," she said. "See you later!" She closed the door.

Maria and Lizzie looked at each other. "Yikes!" said Maria.

"Mom's not usually like that," Lizzie said. "It's just — " She nodded down at Pugsley.

"Are you kidding? Your mom is great!" Maria said. "I doubt *my* mom would put up with a dog like Pugsley for even one day."

Lizzie put Pugsley down, and they started to walk down the street. Pugsley pulled and tugged and lunged on the leash, dashing from one side to another so he could sniff every single smell he came across.

What's that? What's that? What's that? Check it out! Check it out! Check it out!

"He sure does have a lot of energy," said Maria.

"Think," Lizzie said. "Think! We have to figure something out. Pugsley would be *miserable* at the shelter. Imagine that energy all bottled up!"

She and Maria looked at Pugsley, imagining

him cooped up in a kennel. They both shook their heads.

When they got to the fenced-in park, Lizzie let Pugsley off the leash so he can run around a little. She and Maria sat on the swings, watching him dash around in circles on the grass.

"I remember when I was little, I used to come here all the time," Lizzie said as she swung gently back and forth. "I would beg Dad to keep pushing me so I could go higher and higher."

"I was the same way!" Maria said. "Then I learned how to pump my feet so I didn't need a push anymore."

"That was the best!" Lizzie said. "I could swing for hours in those days."

They looked at each other and smiled. Then Lizzie backed way up and pushed into the swing, letting it carry her forward in a high arc. The wind rushed through her hair. "Yahoo!" she yelled, pumping her feet so she went even higher the next time. Maria was swinging, too.

"I could swing higher than anyone else in second grade, except for Will Garrett," Lizzie boasted. "Nobody could swing higher than Will Garrett. Or run faster. Or get into more trouble. Will was always on the move. He kind of drove the teachers crazy."

"We had a boy like that in my school, too. Todd Little. He was always acting up in class. My teacher used to say, 'Ignore him. Todd only wants attention,'" Maria said, in a teacher-y voice. "I always thought that was weird. Like, if Todd wants attention, maybe we should just *give* him some. Then he wouldn't have to do things like empty the pencil sharpener into the fish tank."

Lizzie stuck out her heels and stopped herself. She popped off the swing and stood staring at her best friend. "Maria!" she said. "That's it! I've got it!"

CHAPTER SEVEN

Maria looked confused. "What?"

Lizzie started talking fast, the way she always did when she was excited. "Pugsley only wants attention. That's why he's so bad! But instead of giving him attention, we keep trying to ignore him. So then he just tries harder and harder to get our attention!" She stared at Maria, then at Pugsley (now he was digging madly in the dirt over by the seesaw), then back at Maria.

Maria looked confused. "Uh-huh," she said. "So —"

"So what if we just *give* him more attention — *before* he can misbehave?" Lizzie could not stop grinning. Her idea was brilliant! She was a genius! She could see herself now, accepting the prize for Dog Trainer of the Year. "It just came to me," she would say in her acceptance speech. She would mention Maria, too, of course. Maria had been there. She deserved at least a little bit of the credit.

"Uh, Lizzie?"

Lizzie was so deep in her daydream that it took her a moment to answer. "Yes?"

"That attention thing? I think Pugsley needs some right now." Maria nodded toward Pugsley, who was busy pulling red petunias out of a flower bed near the park's front gate.

Wheee! Look at me! This is the most fun ever! Look at the pretty flowers. Watch the dirt fly. Wheee!

"Oops!" Lizzie jumped off her swing and sprinted toward Pugsley. She didn't yell at him for what he was doing. She just scooped him up and nuzzled his soft, wrinkly face. "Hey, you," she said into his ear. "You're about to get as much attention as you can stand!" She sat down on the grass and started patting Pugsley. "Who's the cutest little Pest?" she cooed. "Who is?"

Maria came over and stuck the plants back into their holes, then patted the soil down around them. "I think they'll be okay." She sat back on her heels and looked at Pugsley, all curled up in Lizzie's lap. "Boy," she said, "I see what you mean. A little attention and he already looks really calm and happy."

"And a calm, happy dog is a *good* dog," Lizzie added. "Let's take him home and throw the tennis ball for him so he can run off some more energy. After that, I'll brush him for a while. And then maybe Charles can read to him." Charles liked to read the comics to Buddy. It had become his favorite Sunday tradition, next to Dad's blueberry pancakes. Even though it wasn't Sunday, he could read the daily comics to Pugsley.

That was the beginning of Operation No More

Mr. Pest, as Charles named it. Over the next week, the whole Peterson family concentrated on giving Pugsley all the attention any dog could crave. Of course, they all made sure to give Buddy lots of attention, too, so he wouldn't be jealous. But Pugsley was the star of the show, and he *loved* the limelight.

One day Lizzie and Maria took Pugsley downtown to meet some of their friends, including Jerry Small, who owned Lucky Dog Books, the best bookstore ever. Jerry had adopted Buddy's mother, Skipper.

"My, my, my! Who's this?" said Jerry when Lizzie and Maria walked in with Pugsley on his leash. Dogs were welcome in Jerry Small's bookstore — in fact, Skipper practically lived there! Jerry knelt down to pat Pugsley. The pug pulled at the leash, putting his paws up on Jerry's knee.

Hi! Hi! Can I kiss you?

"Pugsley!" Lizzie said. "Be good!" She was trying to teach him to say hello without jumping up and licking people's faces.

Jerry called for Skipper, and a bigger version of Buddy came trotting out from behind the counter. "Skipper, meet Pugsley!" said Jerry. Pugsley was still licking Jerry's face, but he stopped for a second to touch noses with Skipper.

Lizzie would have loved to browse in the bookstore, but she didn't. Instead, she stayed close to Pugsley, making sure he got plenty of attention. He behaved very, very well — at least until Jerry gave him a dog biscuit. That made him so happy that he had to jump around a little bit, and he knocked over a display of calendars.

Another day, Charles and Lizzie took Pugsley to meet Mrs. Peabody, an elderly woman who lived at a place called The Meadows. Mrs. Peabody and Charles had met when they were members of Grandbuddies, a program at school where kids had older people for special friends. Mrs. Peabody had adopted one of the Petersons' first foster puppies, a fluffy little white terrier named Snowball.

Mrs. Peabody thought Pugsley was "delightful!" but Snowball wasn't so sure. He barked and barked at Pugsley. Snowball did not want Mrs. Peabody paying attention to any other dogs. Lizzie could understand that. She couldn't quite remember, but she probably felt the same way when she was two years old and Mom and Dad had brought baby Charles home from the hospital. If Lizzie had been a dog, she might have barked at the new little person who was taking up her parents' time.

So Lizzie patted Snowball, but she still made sure that Pugsley got most of her attention. Pugsley got lots of attention from other residents at The Meadows, too. Everybody thought he was the cutest thing ever, and he behaved very nicely — if you didn't count the moment when he chewed on one man's cane . . . or stole another man's scarf.

The next day, Dad and Lizzie took Pugsley down to the fire station to meet Dad's fellow firefighters as well as Gunnar, the dalmatian who was the fire station mascot. That visit went well, except for when Pugsley jumped on Gunnar's back as if he wanted the bigger dog to take him for a ride. Gunnar didn't like that too much. The firefighters thought Pugsley was the funniest thing ever, and they picked him up and passed him around until he struggled to get down.

But best of all was the way Mom figured out how to keep Pugsley out of trouble by giving him plenty of attention when the rest of the family wasn't around. Since Mom mostly worked at home, writing news stories for the *Littleton News*, she and Pugsley spent lots of time together. When Lizzie came home from school one day, she saw that Mom had popped Pugsley into the carrier she had used to keep the Bean close when he was a little baby. It was like a soft backpack that strapped to the front of Mom's chest. Even though he couldn't run and play when he was strapped in, Pugsley *loved* being in that carrier. "He's practically purring!" Mom told Lizzie. She smiled down at the pug puppy as she stroked his wrinkly head.

Oh, it's so cozy in here! I don't have to do any-thing at all to get attention. All I have to do is relax! I think I'll take another little nap. . . .

By the time Wednesday rolled around again, Pugsley had calmed down so much that nobody was calling him Mr. Pest anymore. Lizzie just hoped he would behave well at Bowser's Backyard. Aunt Amanda was going to be amazed at what a good puppy he had turned into. She might even invite him (and Lizzie!) to Camp Bowser for the weekend!

There was only one bad part about the whole thing. Pugsley was learning how to behave, so that meant it was time to start finding him a forever home. The Petersons were only his foster family, after all. Someday soon they were going to have to say good-bye to Mr. Pest — for good.

CHAPTER EIGHT

"Good luck!" Mom leaned over to give Lizzie a kiss as she dropped her and Pugsley off at Bowser's Backyard after school on Wednesday.

"Thanks! We'll probably need it." Lizzie looked down at Pugsley, who was nestled in her arms. He looked so innocent! But Lizzie knew better. Even though his behavior had improved a lot over the last week, Pugsley was still not one hundred percent perfect. He still had his Mr. Pest moments!

Lizzie was just hoping that nothing terrible would happen that afternoon while Aunt Amanda was watching. More than anything, she wanted Aunt Amanda to invite her and Pugsley along to Camp Bowser that weekend. She had dreamed about it all week long. Now, Lizzie waved as Mom drove off. Then, as she walked Pugsley up to the door of the doggy day care, Lizzie gave the little pug a pep talk.

"You can do it, Pugsley. I *know* you can," she said. "You're a good, good puppy. You have behaved yourself all week long. Well, mostly. Except for a few slips here and there, when you weren't getting enough attention. You know, like when you ate Dad's fishing magazine, or when you knocked over Mom's favorite lamp and made her cry. And — well, enough about the slips." Lizzie looked down at Pugsley. "Look, all you have to do is be good for three hours. That equals" — she thought for a minute, doing the multiplication in her mind — "one hundred and eighty minutes of goodness."

Pugsley tugged on his leash, pulling Lizzie toward the door. He snorted impatiently.

Let's go! She keeps talking, and talking, and talking. Blah, blah, blah. When are we going to go inside and see all my friends?

Lizzie laughed. "Okay, you're right. It's time to go in. Just remember — whether or not we get invited to Camp Bowser depends on *you*. Got it?"

Pugsley cocked his head as if he was trying to understand. Lizzie laughed again. "I know you'll do your best. Here we go!" She pushed the door open and she and Pugsley walked in.

"Well! Look who's here!" Aunt Amanda spotted them and came right over. She gave Lizzie a quick hug, then bent down to say hello to Pugsley.

Pugsley did not jump up to lick Aunt Amanda's face. He did not put his paws on her legs. He did not whirl around in excited circles. He just sat down the way Lizzie had taught him, with his curly tail quivering, and held up one paw for a shake.

"My goodness! What a little gentleman!" Aunt Amanda smiled at Pugsley and gave him a scratch between the ears. She looked up at Lizzie. "Your father told me how hard you've all been working with Pugsley. It really shows!"

Lizzie felt her heart swell with pride as she looked down at Pugsley. "No more Mr. Pest!" she said. "Mostly."

"That's just great." Aunt Amanda stood up. "Maybe Pugsley is almost ready for a trip to Camp Bowser!"

That was exactly what Lizzie was hoping to hear. But as soon as she heard it, she started to worry. What if Pugsley messed up? She smiled at her aunt and held up one hand, fingers crossed. "What's today's activity?" she asked as Aunt Amanda led the way into the playroom.

"Paw painting!" Aunt Amanda said over her shoulder.

Lizzie groaned, but not loudly enough for her aunt to hear. This was not good news. Paw painting with dogs was just like finger painting with kids. Only even messier. There were so many ways that Pugsley could get into trouble. Why couldn't it have been Story Day, when all the helpers read to the dogs, or even Field Day, when they had races outside and the dogs got to run around a lot and burn off energy?

Oh, well. Lizzie would just have to stick close to Pugsley and make sure that he had all the attention he needed. That might mean that she wasn't helping as much with the other dogs, but she was sure Aunt Amanda would understand.

The playroom was full of dogs. Fiona was there, and Max, and even Hoss ambled out of the nap room. Hoss loved paw painting.

Aunt Amanda and her helpers had unrolled a long sheet of newsprint that stretched from one end of the room to the other. Now they were putting out paper bowls full of red, yellow, and blue poster paint. They were also trying to get the dogs to settle down and choose a place along the newsprint where they would each make their own paw painting.

Pugsley was tugging at his leash again, but Lizzie did not let him go. She was sure that if she did, he would tear all around the room and leave red, yellow, and blue paw prints everywhere. "Oh, no, you don't," she said. She led him over to a spot next to Hoss, and let the two dogs sniff and wag and say hello. They looked so cute together! The Great Dane was about ten times as big as Pugsley, but he was always gentle and kind to the little pug.

"Okay, everyone!" Amanda called over the sound of happy barking. "Let's start painting!"

Lizzie helped Pugsley dip one front paw into the blue paint, then press it onto the paper. "Fun, isn't it?" she asked him. So far, so good. The old Pugsley would have already run up and down the whole paper three times. The new Pugsley was settled in, enjoying himself. Lizzie noticed that Aunt Amanda was watching. They smiled at each other and Aunt Amanda gave Lizzie a big thumbs-up.

Next to Lizzie, Hoss had dunked each huge front paw into a different color. He was making swoopy paw-strokes in red and yellow. "Nice!" Lizzie said to him. She let go of Pugsley's leash for a second and reached over to wipe Hoss's paws with a paper towel. "Why don't you try some blue?" She pushed the bowl of blue paint over to the Great Dane, and Hoss dipped one big paw into it.

"Hey!" Aunt Amanda yelled. "Watch out for Pugsley!"

Lizzie turned around just in time to see Pugsley putting his whole face down into the yellow paint. "Oh, no!" she cried. One second without attention, and look what he had done! Startled, Pugsley looked up at her. Yellow paint ran down his face, and he stuck out his tongue to taste it. Then he sat down the way she had taught him — right into the red paint! He held up one blue paw.

What? Why are you looking at me like that? Did I do something wrong?

Lizzie groaned. No Camp Bowser for Mr. Pest! She was sure they had blown their big chance.

But Lizzie had a surprise coming to her. At the end of the day, Aunt Amanda came over to give Pugsley his good-bye treat, a little dog biscuit. Then she gave Lizzie a big hug. "Pugsley wasn't perfect," Amanda said.

"I know," Lizzie said miserably. "That paint thing —"

"That wasn't so terrible," Aunt Amanda said. "Pugsley's behavior has really improved. You've worked hard, and you deserve a reward. If it's all right with your mom and dad, how about you and Pugsley come up to Camp Bowser this weekend?"

CHAPTER NINE

"Are we almost —"

"Lizzie? What did I tell you?" Aunt Amanda smiled into the rearview mirror. "No more asking if we're almost there! It won't be long now, I promise."

Lizzie smiled back at her aunt and pretended to zip her lips. But she knew it would be hard to keep from asking again. She could not *believe* that she was finally going to Camp Bowser. But there she was, in the backseat of the Bowser Mobile, behind Aunt Amanda and Uncle James. And behind *her* were six dogs, including Aunt Amanda's three, plus Pugsley, Fiona, and Max, whose owners were away for the weekend.

Lizzie looked out the window at the scenery whizzing by and thought back to Wednesday, when Aunt Amanda invited her and Pugsley to camp. After that, Thursday and Friday seemed to last for years, decades, even centuries! Lizzie had never known two days to go by so slowly, not even the two days before Christmas. But finally, on Friday evening right after supper, the Bowser Mobile pulled up in front of the Petersons' house.

Everybody came outside to see Lizzie and Pugsley off. Charles was pouting a little because he didn't get to go. Luckily, the Bean was too young to really understand. If he knew what Camp Bowser was all about, he would have been *sobbing*. While Uncle James loaded Pugsley into the van, Dad and Aunt Amanda did their special secret handshake from when they were kids, and Mom gave Lizzie a big hug. "Have a *great* time!" she whispered into Lizzie's ear. "And keep an eye on Mr. Pest."

Lizzie didn't need to be reminded. She wanted to make sure she got invited back to Camp Bowser again and again. She was going to make sure the pug was on his best behavior all weekend. She planned to keep on giving him plenty of attention, since that really seemed to work wonders.

Now, in the van, Aunt Amanda met Lizzie's eyes again. "Lizzie," she said. "Now that Pugsley is behaving so much better, don't you think it's time to work on finding him a forever home?"

Lizzie sighed. "I guess so," she said. "I mean, I know you're right. But I'm going to hate to see him go. He's really a great little dog." She pulled a digital camera out of her backpack. "I'm going to take lots of pictures, so I can make a poster when I get home." Lizzie was famous in her family for being really good at using the computer to make posters and signs. Whenever they had a foster puppy who needed a home, Lizzie made a creative poster to put up around town.

"Good idea," said Uncle James, turning to look at Lizzie. "That cute little pug face ought to get some attention."

"He is awfully cute," agreed Aunt Amanda. "I mean, all pugs are adorable, but there's something special about Pugsley."

Lizzie sat back in her seat and tried to concentrate on ideas for Pugsley's poster, instead of on when they would get to Camp Bowser. She was almost surprised when the van stopped a little while later and Aunt Amanda announced, "We're here!"

Lizzie climbed out of the van and took a deep breath of the crisp, cool country air. It was dark out, but a shiny half-moon and thousands of bright stars lit up the sky. Lizzie could smell pine needles and, when she listened for a moment, she could hear the sound of a rushing brook. Aunt Amanda and Uncle James's cabin stood in a clearing, looking cozy and welcoming. Lizzie smiled to herself. She knew she was going to love Camp Bowser.

Uncle James opened the back of the van. "Awww!" he said.

Aunt Amanda and Lizzie came to look. All the dogs were fast asleep in their cages. Pugsley and the two other pugs were sharing a cage, and they were tangled up in one warm, soft, pug-pile. When Pugsley heard their voices, he opened one eye and looked sleepily up at them, wrinkling his velvety black forehead.

"Awww!" said Lizzie and Aunt Amanda.

"I've never seen Lionel and Jack quite so comfortable around another pug," Aunt Amanda whispered. "I almost hate to wake them all up."

But by then, all the dogs were stirring. Lizzie helped Uncle James and Aunt Amanda get all the dogs walked and then settled onto the Pooch Porch, a screened-in sleeping area that was covered wall-to-wall with comfy mattresses, pillows, and blankets. Then Lizzie got into bed in the guest room, sure that she was too excited about being at camp to *ever* fall asleep — and fell asleep instantly.

Camp Bowser turned out to be just as much fun as Lizzie had always dreamed it would be. Saturday started with homemade banana-walnut muffins for people and meat-loaf muffins for dogs. After breakfast, Lizzie and Aunt Amanda took all the dogs down to the stream. The big dogs swam in the deeper part of the stream while the pugs splashed and played in the shallow area.

Pugsley *loved* chasing sticks that Lizzie threw into the water. He dog-paddled frantically, grunting and snorting happily as he raced Lionel and Jack for his prize. Then all three pugs climbed up onto the bank of the stream and shook off, spraying Lizzie and Aunt Amanda with cold water and making them shriek.

After their swim, Lizzie and Aunt Amanda took all the dogs for a long hike through the big, fenced-in area around the cottage. By the time they got back, the dogs were nearly dry, and Uncle James had a snack waiting. After that, they did arts and crafts, making paw prints in clay to take home to their owners. Then it was time for doggy massages, followed by naps on the Pooch Porch, followed by lunch.

In the afternoon the dogs took another hike, played some more in the brook, and bounced on the trampoline. While Aunt Amanda made dinner, there was music time, when Uncle James played the guitar and sang songs about dogs. Lizzie kept her camera with her all day and took dozens of pictures of Pugsley enjoying himself with his new best pals.

Pugsley was getting plenty of attention, and all the activities kept him busy. He was behaving perfectly! Lizzie was starting to think that Mr. Pest was really gone for good — until Sunday afternoon.

Pugsley seemed extra-sleepy at nap time, so

Lizzie left him alone on the Pooch Porch while she and Uncle James played with the other dogs. Big mistake. Aunt Amanda was the one who discovered the little pug in the middle of his wild rampage. "Pugsley!" she yelled when she saw what he had done. Lizzie and Uncle James ran in to see.

"Oh, no!" Lizzie could not believe her eyes. How could one little dog make such a huge mess in so short a time? Every blanket and pillow and mattress on the porch had been shredded. Feathers filled the air. And Pugsley lay in the middle of it all, looking up at them with innocent eyes.

I was bored! I was lonely! So I had a little fun. What did you expect?

Uncle James looked like he wanted to laugh.

Aunt Amanda shook her head. "Mr. Pest returns," was all she said. Then she handed Lizzie a broom and a garbage bag.

It was a quiet ride home that night in the Bowser Mobile. Lizzie knew that Aunt Amanda was very disappointed in Pugsley. Lizzie was, too. Just when he was starting to seem like the kind of dog that anyone would want, he went back to his old tricks. How was Lizzie *ever* going to find Pugsley a forever home?

CHAPTER TEN

Back at home, Lizzie kept a close eye on Pugsley. After school on Monday and Tuesday, he stayed in her room with her while she worked on a poster. WANTED! her poster said at the top. In the middle was a big picture of Pugsley, looking innocent and adorable. Underneath the picture it said, "Wanted: a very good home for an occasionally naughty puppy. Name: Pugsley. Sometimes known as Mr. Pest." Then there were four other pictures of Pugsley playing at camp. Maybe the funny poster would help find the right home for Pugsley, with people who understood that he was just a puppy, and that a puppy wasn't always perfect.

Lizzie was not planning to take Pugsley to

Bowser's Backyard on Wednesday. She had a feeling that Aunt Amanda had just about had enough of the pesky pug. Instead, she planned to spend the afternoon putting up posters, with Maria's help. That was why she was surprised when the phone rang after dinner on Tuesday and Mom said it was Aunt Amanda, calling for Lizzie. "Just checking to make sure you're bringing Pugsley to day care tomorrow!" her aunt said when Lizzie came to the phone.

"Really? We can come?" Lizzie asked.

"Really," said Aunt Amanda. "I'm counting on your help here, and — well, to be honest, I miss that little Mr. Pest."

"I promise he'll behave," Lizzie said.

Aunt Amanda laughed. "I'm not sure anybody can promise that. But I will expect you to keep a close eye on him and give him lots of attention."

"I will," vowed Lizzie.

And she did. She watched Pugsley like a hawk all afternoon. And she noticed that Aunt Amanda was watching, too. Every time Lizzie looked up, there was Aunt Amanda, checking on Pugsley. Even though Bowser's Backyard was very, very busy that day, Aunt Amanda was always watching.

It made Lizzie nervous.

Lizzie knew Pugsley already had more than three strikes against him. If he did something *really* naughty, Aunt Amanda would probably kick him out for good. And if Pugsley couldn't spend at least one afternoon a week at Bowser's Backyard, Lizzie knew Mom would probably run out of patience and kick him out of the *house*! Pugsley would end up at Caring Paws, stuck in a cage while he waited for someone to adopt him — *if* the shelter even had room. Lately they had been totally full. Where would Pugsley go then?

It would be so much better if Lizzie could find Pugsley a forever home. She had brought her signs to show Aunt Amanda, but her aunt would be way too busy to look at them until later, after most of the dogs had been picked up by their owners.

It was a special day at Bowser's Backyard: bath day! For an extra fee, Amanda and her helpers would give any dog a bath. Lizzie knew better than to let Pugsley anywhere near the tub room. Pugsley plus water usually equaled trouble.

Even so, Mr. Pest showed up a few times before the afternoon was over.

The first time was right after Aunt Amanda had given her own pugs, Lionel and Jack, their baths. While Lizzie was helping to dry Jack off, Pugsley convinced Lionel that it would be fun to run out the doggy door and roll around in the muddy play yard.

Come on! Come on! You smell too good. Don't you want to smell like a dog again? Let's go play!

Then, while Lizzie was helping with Lionel's *second* bath, Pugsley and Jack got into a wrestling match underneath the bunk bed in the nap room where it was all dusty.

Ah-choo! Ah-choo! I'b got subthig id by dose. . . .

Lizzie thought it was actually kind of cute that the three pugs seemed to like one another so much. And Aunt Amanda seemed to agree. At least, she didn't get *too* mad at Pugsley, who could not stop sneezing. She just smiled and shook her head. "Pugs will be pugs!" she said as she picked them up and took them into the tub room for another quick rinse.

After that, Lizzie brought Pugsley into the playroom, where Amanda's helpers were keeping the other dogs busy with a game of find-the-biscuit. While Lizzie was helping to tuck biscuits here and there under chairs or beneath pillows, Pugsley managed to find the whole *box* of biscuits. Just when Aunt Amanda came in to see how the game was going, he nudged the box over with his nose, tossing biscuits all over the floor for all the dogs to snap up.

Yay! Look what I did! Aren't I the smartest little dog ever???

It was a long afternoon. Lizzie was exhausted by the time Aunt Amanda turned the sign on the window to CLOSED and locked the front door of Bowser's Backyard.

Lizzie plopped down on a chair, holding Pugsley in her arms. Aunt Amanda came over to sit next to her.

"You saw everything, didn't you?" Lizzie asked miserably.

Aunt Amanda nodded. "Pugsley isn't perfect yet," she said. "He still has some growing up to do. But you found the key to helping him behave better. All he needs is attention, and plenty of it."

Then she changed the subject. "Didn't you have something to show me, Lizzie?" she asked. "Some signs you made?"

Lizzie opened her backpack and pulled out the signs. She sighed as she handed one to Aunt Amanda. "I hope we can find Pugsley a home."

Aunt Amanda looked down at the sign in her hand. "This is cute," she said. Then, slowly, she ripped it in half and handed the two pieces back to Lizzie. "But I don't think you should put it up."

Lizzie gasped. "What? Why not?"

"Because Uncle James and I talked it over last night. We realized that we've fallen in love with Pugsley, even if he *is* sometimes a pest. Lionel and Jack love him, too. I was watching him all day today before I made my final decision."

"You mean, about kicking him out?" Lizzie asked. She was a little confused.

"No, about adopting him. We've decided to be a *three*-pug family." She reached out to gather

Pugsley into her arms. "What do you think about that, Pugsley?"

Pugsley snorted and snuffled and sneezed. Then he licked Aunt Amanda's chin.

Lizzie laughed. "I think that means 'yes, please!'" she said. She sat back in her chair and sighed happily as she watched her aunt cuddle with the little pug. Pugsley had found a perfect home with someone who could give him all the attention he needed and deserved. He would have two big pug brothers to play with and teach him manners. And the best part was, Lizzie would get to see him all the time — at Bowser's Backyard *and* at Camp Bowser!

PUPPY TIPS

Some puppies have a LOT of energy! It can be very hard to teach them the manners they need to be good pets and happy family members. Be patient! Sometimes a puppy just needs to grow up a little. Other times he or she needs lots and lots of special attention, just like Pugsley did. All puppies do best when they know they are loved.

It's also important for everybody in the family to treat the puppy the same way, and with the same rules. If your brother lets the puppy jump up on him when you and your parents are trying to teach the puppy *not* to jump up, the puppy will be confused.

Don't forget that puppy kindergarten classes can be a great place for your pet to learn manners — and for you and your family to learn how to be good pet owners.

Dear Reader:

When Django was a little puppy, I took him to puppy kindergarten. He learned to play well with other puppies and he also learned things like how to sit, lie down, and walk on a leash. But he was a naughty puppy sometimes! Once he chewed a hole in my favorite rug. He would also steal food whenever he had the chance! Still, when Django got older, he turned into a very good dog.

Yours from the Puppy Place,
Ellen Miles

P.S. If you enjoyed reading about a dog who loves to chew things, check out CODY, another pup whose teeth take charge!

THE PUPPY PLACE
Where every puppy finds a home
CODY
113
ELLEN MILES
SCHOLASTIC

DON'T MISS THE NEXT
PUPPY PLACE ADVENTURE!

Here's a peek at MAGGIE AND MAX!

"Eatalotta, eatalotta, eatalotta pizza!"

"Pepperoni, mushrooms, anchovies on the pizza,"

"Mozzarella cheese and Parmesan, too!"

"Mmmm, mmmm, good!"

Charles shouted happily with the group. He loved the pizza chant. He loved his bright yellow T-shirt. He loved working toward his Wolf rank.

In fact, Charles loved just about everything about being in Cub Scouts.

It was cool that his best friend Sammy was in his den. It was awesome that they would both soon become Wolves. And Charles thought it was most especially super cool *and* awesome that his mom and dad were Akelas — that is, den leaders. That meant that all six Cub Scouts in Charles's den came to the Petersons' house for their meeting every week, and it also meant that both Mom and Dad came along to the Scout's monthly pack meeting.

After Charles's dad finished leading the pizza chant, his mom shooed the pack out to the backyard so they could practice for the "Feats of Skill" they would have to perform as part of their Wolf Badge requirements. Charles and Sammy were practicing their front and back rolls when Charles looked up and saw a furry brown face watching from a window in the house. "Hi, Buddy!" he yelled, waving to his puppy.

Charles loved Buddy so much. More than ice

cream, more than Cub Scouts, maybe even more than Christmas, which was only a few weeks away — that's how much Charles loved his puppy. Buddy was brown with a white, heart-shaped patch on his chest. He was the cutest, smartest, funniest, softest, sweetest puppy ever, and — best of all — he belonged to the Petersons for ever and ever.

Now, in the upstairs window, another little face popped up next to Buddy's. That was the Bean, Charles's little brother. (His name was really Adam, but nobody *ever* called him that.) The Bean had a fuzzy green stuffed turtle hanging from his mouth. Mr. Turtle came from the pet store, and he had a squeaker inside. He was really a toy for dogs, not for little boys. But the Bean was not exactly a regular little boy. The Bean loved to pretend that he was a dog.

Then, a third face popped up. It was Lizzie, Charles's older sister. She was keeping an eye on Buddy and the Bean while the den had its meeting. Charles figured that Lizzie was probably a little jealous of all the special time he got with Mom and Dad during Scout meetings, and all the fun things the Scouts got to do, like crafts and skits and games.

Sure enough, Lizzie stuck her tongue out at Charles. He stuck his tongue out back at her. Lizzie put her pinkies in the corners of her mouth and pulled it into a jack-o'-lantern shape. Charles did the same back at her. Charles was thinking about trying a new face with crossed eyes and a dangling tongue, when he heard Mom's voice.

"Okay, Scouts, let's head inside!" Mom was by the back door, waving her arms. "Our visitor has arrived and it's time to sit down and put on our listening ears."

The den often had special visitors who talked about their jobs or about how the Scouts could make a difference. Last month, the chief of police had come! He had made all the Scouts "official deputies." That was cool.

Back in the living room, Dad was standing next

to the Christmas tree talking to a tall man with a big, round stomach. Dad must have said something funny because just as Charles and the others came in, the man burst into a loud, happy laugh. Dad was laughing, too.

But both men got more serious once the Scouts had settled down and were sitting in a circle on the floor. "This is Mr. Baker," Dad said, introducing the man. "He is the director of the Nest, which is a shelter for families who need temporary homes."

"You mean, like the puppies we take care of?" Charles asked.

Dad nodded. "Sort of. Does everybody remember the big fire at Pinewood Apartments last week?"

Charles nodded along with all the other boys. He sure did remember. He remembered Dad's beeper going off in the middle of dinner. Dad was a fireman, and he was always ready to go in an emergency. The Pinewood fire had kept him busy until very late that night.

"Fortunately, nobody was hurt by that fire," Mr. Baker said. "But three families lost their homes. So they are staying with us at the Nest. We have two other families staying there, too, families that need a little help. With five families, we're full to the brim."

Sammy raised his hand. "How long do the people stay?"

"Usually only for a month or two," answered Mr. Baker. "Just until they get back on their feet. Sometimes a mom or dad needs some help with finding a job, or with learning English if they are from another country. We can help with that. We also help the kids with their homework, and make sure they get to school every day."

Now another Scout spoke up. "Do the families help out at the Nest?"

"They sure do," said Mr. Baker. "We all work together to keep the Nest going, just like you all help out with chores at home. In return, the families get a safe, warm place to live, and three meals a day until they can find new homes."

Now Mom spoke up. "Three *delicious* meals," she said. "I had dinner there once when I was writing an article about the Nest." Charles's mom was a reporter for the *Littleton News*, the local newspaper.

"We do have a good cook," agreed Mr. Baker. "And I must admit I enjoy helping out in the kitchen, too. I wonder if you boys can guess what kind of things I like to make? I'll give you a hint. My name says it all."

Charles got the hint. "Cookies!" he yelled.

"Cake!" yelled Sammy.

"That's right, I'm a baker," said Mr. Baker. "And when you come to the Nest next week, you can sample some of my treats."

Dad spoke up again. "Remember how we agreed at our last meeting that we wanted to volunteer somewhere, to help others in our community? Well, Mr. Baker has invited us to help serve dinner at the Nest one night a week. We'll even be there for Christmas Eve!"

Charles thought it sounded like fun. Until he heard what came next.

Mr. Baker was nodding and smiling. "We can't wait to have you," he said. "Especially on Christmas Eve. That's when we put on our annual showcase — you know, singing, dancing, all that stuff. And our volunteers are the stars!"

Charles gulped. Performing in front of a group of people was *not* his idea of fun. Just the thought of it made his hands feel all hot and sweaty. But there wasn't time to worry about that now. It was time to say good-bye to Mr. Baker and finish up their meeting with a song. Mom turned out all the lights except for the Christmas tree lights. Then, Charles and the other Scouts sang *"Show Akela we stand tall, we are Cub Scouts after all"* to the tune of "It's a Small World After All." Singing was fun, as long as it wasn't for an audience.

They were on the last verse when Charles heard

the phone ring. A moment later, Lizzie rushed into the room. "Ms. Dobbins just called!" she said to Mom. "She wants us to come over right away. She says she needs a foster family *tonight*."

Ms. Dobbins was the director of Caring Paws, the animal shelter where Lizzie volunteered one day a week. She and her staff took care of lots of dogs and cats, but sometimes they needed help. That's where the Petersons came in.

As soon as the last Cub Scout had been picked up by his parents, the Petersons piled into their van and headed for Caring Paws. When they arrived at the animal shelter, Ms. Dobbins greeted them at the door. Then, without wasting any time, she led them down the hall. Charles thought they were going to the dog room, but instead she brought them into her office. There, in the corner, was an enormous cardboard box. It was wrapped in bright green shiny paper, and a big red floppy bow hung down one side.

"Look what just arrived," said Ms. Dobbins.

"I was working late and I didn't even hear a car pull up, but when I went to lock the front door I found this box on the steps."

Charles and Lizzie and the Bean moved closer to the box and peeked inside. Their parents were right behind them.

Charles caught a glimpse of a wide, shaggy, white-and-brown face with big eyes that looked like melting chocolate kisses. A puppy! A puppy with floppy brown ears and a long feathery tail and the biggest paws Charles had ever seen.

"Wow!" Dad was staring into the box. "That is one *huge* puppy!"

"Ohh!" said Lizzie. "How cute! Is it a Saint Bernard?"

"Uppy!" whispered the Bean, who had to stand on his tiptoes to look into the box.

"Keep looking," said Ms. Dobbins.

"Oh, my!" said Mom suddenly. "There's a kitten in there, too!"

ABOUT THE AUTHOR

Ellen Miles likes to write about the different personalities of dogs. She is the author of more than 28 books, including the Puppy Place and Taylor-Made Tales series as well as *The Pied Piper* and other Scholastic Classics. Ellen loves to be outdoors every day, walking, biking, skiing, or swimming, depending on the season. She also loves to read, cook, explore her beautiful state, and hang out with friends and family. She lives in Vermont.

If you love animals, be sure to read all the adorable stories in the Puppy Place series!